Beverly Jenkins

Copyright

Crystal Clear

Book ISBN: 978-1979825290

NYLA Publishing
350 7th Avenue, Suite 2003, NY 10001, New York.
http://www.nyliterary.com

CHAPTER ONE

Crystal couldn't take it anymore. If she had to stay in Henry Adams Kansas one more minute she'd explode. Yeah, it was great being seventeen and having a big beautiful bedroom, wearing the best clothes and flying around in a white jet, but she missed the life she'd led in Dallas before being adopted by Ms. Bernadine Brown and she wanted it back.

She dragged her largest suitcase out of the closet. Handling it brought back memories of the places she'd visited with her new mom, like Spain, Italy, LA and the off the chain times they'd shared, but pampered Henry Adams living was turning her into someone she wasn't sure she knew how to be or wanted to be. The old Crystal was up on the latest dances, street slang and which clubs had the best-looking guys. Present day Crystal was clueless on all that. Old Crystal loved burgers and hot salty fries. The new one ate salmon, salads with balsamic vinaigrette and five grain bread.

Deciding the big case wasn't the best choice for a girl needing to travel light, she opted for her back pack instead. For now, all she needed was one or two changes of clothing, a few toiletries and her hair stuff and she'd be good. Once she got to Dallas, she'd have her best friend Kiki put her up until she found a waitressing job. With money in her pocket she'd be able to afford a place of her own and start her new life. Opening her dresser drawers, she took out a couple of cute tops, some socks and underwear. She'd just stuffed the items in the backpack when she noticed ten-year-old Zoey Garland watching her from the doorway. So much for leaving town without anyone knowing. "Hey, Zoe." Zoey lived two doors down, and like Crystal, was one of the foster kids brought to Henry Adams by Ms. Bernadine Brown.

"Where're you going?"

"Away. And I need you to keep it to yourself."

"Why?"

"Because I don't want anybody trying to change my mind."

Zoey eyed her for a moment. "Don't you like us anymore?"

The sincerity fed Crystal's inner guilt and she gritted out, "I just have to go, okay? Stop asking a million questions."

"Okay," she whispered.

The sadness on the small face made Crystal wish she'd been nicer. Never in her life had she expected to love a little white girl like a sister, but they had a bond tight as blood. Leaving this way was going to cause a lot of hurt all the way around, but she didn't want to deal with that now.

"Are you ever coming back?"

Crystal crossed to her low-slung dresser with its big mirror. Sticking her flat iron and other hair stuff into the now bulging pack, she shook her head. Zoey was reflected in the mirror and Crystal did her best to ignore the sheen of tears in her eyes. "I'll call when I get where I'm going. Promise."

When Zoey ran across the room, arms spread wide, Crystal grabbed her up and held on tight. She tried to pretend she wasn't crying too, but the tears ran down her cheeks unchecked. "It's now your job to keep Amari and the rest of the knuckleheads in line. Okay?"

"Please stay here."

Crystal stepped back. "I gotta go, or I'm going to lose

my mind. I love Ms. Bernadine and everybody, but you remember how it was on the street?" She was looking forward to the freedom, the fun and hanging with her friends.

"All I remember is having no place to live and my mom stealing food so I could eat."

"It isn't going to be like that. I have friends where I'm going, I'll be fine, and like I said, I'll call. And you have to promise you won't tell."

Zoey's lips tightened.

"Promise me, Zo."

After a few moments, she acquiesced, albeit reluctantly. "Okay."

Crystal knew Zoey would tell eventually- she was a little kid, but Crystal planned to be well on her way to Dallas by the time that happened.

Zoey wiped at her tears with her hands. "Are you going to walk?"

"No." Crystal glanced around her room. The sadness that grabbed her from having to leave her art supplies, along with the rest of the wonderful things that defined her life in Henry Adams was almost overwhelming. Equally painful was the sight of the easels holding the two finished paintings of the triptych she'd been working on a for an upcoming art competition in LA. That the project would never be finished added its weight to the turmoil churning inside, but she shook it off and focused on Dallas. "I have someone driving me to the highway. Then I'll hitch."

"That's dangerous!"

Crystal sighed. Zoey had way more adult in her than any other little kid she knew. "I'll be fine."

"No, you won't!"

Crystal eyed her. "Go home."

It was Friday night and everyone in town was over at the rec center watching the movies. Why Zoey wasn't there,

Crys didn't know and didn't have time to hear the reason. She was centered on leaving, and the sooner she did, the sooner she'd feel better.

Zoey watched silently.

"What?" Crystal demanded.

She shook her head and replied quietly, "Nothing. I'm going home. Bye, Crystal."

"Bye, Zoey." Throat thick with emotion, she watched Zoey and her green tennis shoes leave the room.

In the silence that followed, she dashed at her tears, took one last look around her beautiful bedroom, pulled on the navy-blue leather jacket she'd gotten for her birthday in LA last year and shrugged on the backpack. Downstairs, she took a moment to tape the short note she'd written to Ms. Bernadine to the front door and closed it softly behind her.

It was dark, but she spotted Zoey standing on her porch under the light. Crystal shook her head at the girl's persistence and got in the waiting car. "Hey Thad."

"Hey, Crys. Ready for your adventure?"

"Yep." Thad Jeffries was in her weekend art class. He liked her a lot, and she'd made sure to cultivate the relationship. They'd gone out a few times and he was really nice. When she told him a few days ago that she had her mom's permission to backpack across the country and needed a ride to the highway, he'd been more than happy to help her out. She knew taking advantage of him wasn't right, but she couldn't've gotten anyone else's support on something like this, so she'd used the gullible country boy instead.

He pulled away from curb. "This is pretty exciting, Crys."

She fastened her seat belt. "Yeah, it is." She knew Zoey was watching but she refused to let it add to her already churning emotions.

"Wish my parents would let me do something like this,

but they're way too stiff. Your mom's pretty special."

"Yes, she is." And leaving this way would break her heart. Crys set that aside and concentrated instead on the dark countryside.

"Do you know where you want to be dropped off?"

"The south exit should be good."

"You got it."

And so, twenty minutes later, Crystal gave Thad a quick peck on the cheek and opened the passenger side door. "Thanks, Thad."

"No problem. Be careful and have fun." With a wave goodbye, he headed back towards town.

Alone, Crystal began walking along the shoulder of Highway 183 with her thumb out and her hopes high.

She walked south for over an hour. Cars and semis whizzed by but no one stopped. A couple of times she had to jump out of the way of trucks that flew by too close, their horns blaring as their wheels churned up gravel that pelted her legs and arms. Each incident left her heart pounding but she kept moving. Her teacher, Mr. James said during the early seventies kids hitchhiked all over the country. When she began formulating her plan to run away, she'd taken that information to heart, but this was so not the seventies and it was night time. She had to be careful accepting a ride.

Not that she got any invitations. The longer she walked the heavier the backpack felt. The straps were cutting into her shoulders and her feet were beginning to hurt, too. She'd opted to wear her new, cinnamon suede boots, knowing they'd impress her Dallas friends, but she should've chosen more comfortable footwear. There was also the danger that the police might ride down on her, so she stuck to the edge of the dark highway as best she could and told herself going back to Dallas was still a good idea.

A check of the illuminated dial on her pricey watch

showed she'd been walking close to two hours. Had Zoey already alerted Ms. Bernadine? Once again, guilt flooded her with the knowledge of how hurt her mom would be. She'd given Crystal everything, most importantly a home filled with love and had her heart set upon sending her adopted daughter off to college when the time came. However, the part of Crystal that was running away kept refusing to see the value in such an experience, even as the other parts wailed at the prospect of the devastating loss.

Telling herself she'd made the right decision, she buried logic and kept walking. A semi blew by, then slowed to a stop. Because she'd been so deep in thought, she hadn't seen the driver's face. When the truck's flashers came on, she supposed the person behind the wheel was waiting for her to catch up. She was really tired of walking, but she didn't want to get in a truck with some crazy. The horn blared, sounding extra loud in the darkness. Her decision made, she ran and prayed this was the right move.

The door opened. To her surprise a thin, glasses wearing Black woman stared down from the driver's seat. "You want a ride?"

"Yes, ma'am."

"Where you headed?"

"South."

"Get in."

After Crystal complied, the lady trucker maneuvered the big eighteen-wheeler back onto the highway. "Your mama know you out here in the middle of the night?"

Crystal lied flippantly, "Yeah."

"Liar."

She froze. "How do you know?"

"Because you're wearing nice clothes and you called me ma'am, which means somebody raised you well."

Crystal didn't respond.

"Running away?"

Silence.

"Makes me no never mind. Just be glad the Good Lord sent *me* to pick you up and not some crazy rapist who'd leave you half naked and sprawled in a ditch somewhere."

Crystal's eyes widened.

The woman turned her way and the wavering lights of the cab played over her sternly set features. "What? You didn't think that could happen?"

"I thought about it, yes."

"But not to you, right?"

Crystal squirmed.

The woman shook her head as if Crystal were dumb and dumber. "Name's Alma by the way. What do you want to be called?"

"Lynn."

"Where south you heading, *Lynn*?" She didn't bother hiding her skeptical tone.

"Dallas."

"That's my destination, too. After that, you're on your own."

Crystal whispered, "Thank you."

"You're welcome."

Tired and grateful, even though Alma reminded her of Henry Adam's matriarch Tamar July, Crystal closed her eyes. Two breaths later she was asleep.

CHAPTER TWO

When she awakened the next morning, it took her a moment to get her bearings. Alma glanced over. "Mornin'"

"Good morning." Crystal's brain was foggy, and her body felt like she'd been turned into a pretzel. She'd never fallen asleep in the seat of a truck before and vowed never to again. "Where are we?"

"Just outside Dallas."

"Already?"

"Only a bit under eight hours from where I picked you up."

"Oh." She peered out the window at the businesses and billboards lining the highway and the ton of cars speeding by in the outer lanes. Civilization!

"Where do you want to be dropped off?"

"Oak Cliff."

Oak Cliff was the "hood", and in response to Alma's disapproving face, Crystal replied firmly, "I know how to take care of myself."

"That why you sporting that big fancy watch?"

Crys's lips thinned. The lady trucker was right but Crys had had just about enough of Alma's Tamar sounding self. She undid the watch and stuck it down into her back pack. The Crystal of old would've known better than to parade around wearing such an eye-popping piece of bling, but she'd been so intent upon showing off, being cautious hadn't crossed her mind. Appalled at how far she'd fallen since living in NoWhereVille Henry Adams, it was yet another example of why she needed to leave the small town behind. She needed to resurrect her hard, old self, because on the streets of Oak Cliff she couldn't afford to be stupid and soft unless she wanted to be prey in a place where two legged predators ruled.

Later, after availing herself of Alma's small, on board restroom, it was time to say goodbye. "Thanks for the ride," she offered as Alma pulled the rig into the parking lot of a Walgreen's.

"You're welcome. Good luck."

Crystal nodded and hopped down to the pavement. After watching the semi reenter the traffic, she set off on foot.

The area was familiar even if some of the landmarks she'd known four years ago were gone: like the Korean nail shop, and the African American bookstore that were once in the now dilapidated looking strip mall she passed. The houses appeared to be more tired than she remembered. Many had plywood over the windows, a sign that they'd been abandoned. There wasn't much traffic, but it was way more than there'd ever been back in Henry Adams. Crossing the street garnered a few short beeps from some of the male drivers trying to hit on her. That hadn't changed. She ignored them and kept walking.

Hunger called, so her first stop was McDonald's. She sat inside, and while downing the hamburgers she'd missed so much, did her best not to stare at the customers. It had been her hope to run across a familiar face, but everyone was a stranger. Her meal done, she dumped her trash and walked out. Across the street stood one of the big chain restaurants. Finding a job was a top priority. Since she was sure her waitressing experience at the Dog back home would be her golden ticket, she headed there.

"We aren't open yet," an older woman called out from where she stood placing small plastic menus on some of the nearby tables. "Come back at eleven."

"I'm looking for a job and was wondering if I could fill out an application?"

Her request caught the attention of the other wait staff personnel, but after giving her a cursory once over they resumed their duties.

The woman walked over. "I'm the manager. Name's Melody." She resembled a crane with glasses. "How old are you?"

"Eighteen," came the lie.

"Do you have any experience?"

"Yes, ma'am. I've been a waitress for about a year."

"Where."

Crystal hesitated a beat. "Kansas City."

Melody assessed her silently. Crystal prayed the lie didn't trip her up, and that her stylish but slightly rumpled appearance wouldn't be held against her.

"Okay. Let me get an application and I'll give you an interview soon as you're done. Had somebody quit yesterday, so I'll need you to start asap."

"That would be great."

Upon Melody's return, the ecstatic Crystal took the application, sat on the bench near the entrance and began filling it out. She penned her name on the top line but paused when the application asked for her address and Social Security number. Using her Henry Adams address was out, and she had no idea what her Social Security number was. The few times she'd needed it in the past, Ms. Bernadine either recited the digits or Crystal copied it directly from the card which was normally kept filed away with all their other important papers. Crystal scanned the rest of the application and saw it also asked for references. Were she still in Henry

Adams that would be easy, but she wasn't, and she'd told Melody she was from Kansas City. Sighing at this first setback, she glanced up to see the manager watching her. Crystal gave her a fake smile and decided a few more lies wouldn't hurt. She put the name of her old high school in the slot that asked where she'd graduated. Made up an address for the restaurant she'd claimed to have worked in previously and wrote random numbers in the spot asking for her Social Security number. After making up names and addresses for the references, she placed her pen in her backpack and walked to the counter.

Melody looked it over. "So, you graduated from Dallas Central last year?"

"Yes, ma'am. I was going to go to college but – "

"I thought you were from Kansas City."

She froze. "I – uh moved there right after I graduated."

"Uh huh."

Crystal fought to remain calm.

"And this is your Social Security number?"

She nodded.

"Recite it for me because there're too many numbers here."

She couldn't remember what she'd written down.

Melody waited.

Crys tried a winning smile "Hand it back. I just got mixed up."

"Recite it please."

When Crystal didn't respond promptly, Melody slowly tore the application in half.

"Wait!" Crys cried as the pieces disappeared into the wastebasket.

"You gave me an obviously bogus Social Security number, and Dallas Central was torn down two and a half years ago. Good bye." With that, Melody walked away, tossing over her shoulder, "And don't bother coming back."

A disgraced Crystal left the restaurant. Totally humiliated, she glanced over at the McDonald's and the other fast food places nearby but figured they'd all ask her for the same information. She never wanted to go through such an embarrassing encounter ever again. Her dream of quickly finding a job was as trashed as that application. Angry at herself for being so clueless about how this stuff worked, she pulled herself together and set out again.

The October day was warm and filled with the smells of fast food and car exhaust instead of manure, animals and open fields like it was in Kansas. Taking in deep breaths of the urban air, she told herself this was how air was supposed to smell. Thoughts of Kansas brought to mind Ms. Bernadine who was probably past frantic with worry. More than likely she'd called County Sheriff Will Dalton for help, but without knowing Crys's true destination they'd be like Cletus the hog chasing his tail. She planned to follow through on her promise to Zoey and call, but for the moment she focused on not feeling down about her unsuccessful job search, and on finding out if her best friend Kelly "Kiki" Page still lived with her mother Estelle.

Her knock was answered by Estelle, who peered out warily through the screen door. 'What do you want?"

"Hi, Ms. Page. Remember me?"

"No."

"Crystal Chambers. I'm a friend of Kiki's."

"She doesn't live here anymore." Ms. Page studied her for a few more seconds then apparently made the connection. "Okay, I remember you now. You used to have that nasty gold weave."

Crys's lips thinned. "Yes." She wouldn't be caught dead with that mess in her hair now.

"I put Kiki out."

"Do you know where she's living?"

"No. Told her to not to come back her until she gets rid of that gang banger Bobby. You look different. Where've you been living?'

"Someplace else. How do I get in touch with her? You have her number?"

"No"

Crystal's balloon of hope began deflating again. "I just got back in town and I'd really like to hook up with her. You know of anybody who might – "

Ms. Page closed the door.

Crys wanted to curse. *Now what*? Dejected, she glanced up and down the street with its worn houses and old cars parked at the curb and tried to come up with a Plan B. It hadn't occurred to her that she might not be able to find her former best friend because life had moved on.

Frustrated, she left the porch and started walking back the way she'd come. Surely, she hadn't come all this way just to go back to living on the street. She'd been relatively good at it once upon a time but preferred not to have to go that route. She had three hundred dollars in her wallet, more than enough to get a cheap motel room to stay in until she could do better.

A slick black Audi with the music bumping loud eased up beside her. The passenger side window slid down and a seductive male voice called out from within. "You need a ride sweet thing?"

Seeing Kiki's cousin Ross Morgan draped over the wheel, filled her with relief. She walked over and leaned into the open window. "Hey, Ross."

His puzzled face was mirrored in his voice. "You know me?"

She rolled her eyes. "Yes. I'm Crystal. Crystal Chambers?"

Turning down the volume, he checked her out again before asking uncertainly, "Kiki's girl, Crystal?"

"Yeah." Despite not being recognized, she was so glad to see a familiar face she could've kissed him.

"You look different." His eyes trailed over her again. "Oh, I know why. You ditched the weave. Damn, you look good girl."

Ross was three years older and a player. Back in the day, he was also the hook-up man. Could get you anything you wanted from an X-Box, to new tires, as long as you didn't ask where the goods originated. She'd also had a crush on him that went back to middle school. "I'm trying to hook up with Kiki. Do you know where she's staying?"

"Yeah. Get in."

While he drove, she tried not to stare his way. He was still chocolate fine. Not as fine as Diego July, but Ross had that urban fine going on. Shaved head. Studs in both ears. He was wearing a blue tee that showed off the black, free form ink tats on his guns. She forced herself to breathe slowly and not act like she'd never been in a nice car with a cute guy before.

When they stopped at a red light, he asked, "So where you been?"

"Kansas City."

"Your man spring for the outfit?"

"No, my mother died," she lied. "Been collecting her social security."

"Ah. Sorry to hear about your moms."

"Thanks. So, what've you been up to?"

"Same ol' this and that. Just trying to make a living. How long you planning on sticking around?"

"Permanently I hope. Need to find a job first though."

"Good luck with that."

"I got skills." Even though she lacked a social security card and a current address.

He gave her the heart melting grin she remembered so well. "I bet you do."

Her melted heart pounded.

"Make me want to kick my own girl to the curb and see just how skilled you are."

"Yeah, right."

"You think I'm lying."

She didn't believe him for a minute. "Who's your lady now?"

"Unique Ralston."

Crystal was stunned by that. When she last lived in Dallas, Unique Ralston had been singing in her pastor daddy's church choir and looking down her nose at poor people like Crystal and Kiki. "Thought she was going to college when she graduated."

"One taste of my loving changed all that," he boasted. "We got a place not too far from Kiki and Bobby."

Although surprised to hear about Ross and the stuck-up Ms. Unique, she wasn't about Kiki and Bobby. They'd been together since sixth grade. "How're they doing?"

He blew out a breath. "Please. I keep telling Bobby he could make some real money hanging with me, but he's stuck on working a bullshit minimum wage job washing cars at a dealership." He shook his head as though finding that choice unfathomable. "He keeps talking about starting his own business. He never even finished high school, and now with the twins. He needs to be out here making stacks instead of chasing smoke."

"Wait. Back up. He and Kiki have twins?"

"Yeah. Almost a year old."

"Wow." Life had most definitely moved on. Kiki was only a year older than Crystal. How in the world was she dealing with twins? Were she and Bobby still hitting the clubs? Crystal hoped so, because it was one of the first things she wanted to do.

As if reading her mind, Ross asked, "So, what you doing tonight?"

"Not sure. I'd like to celebrate being back. Is the Grind still open?"

"Nah. Burned down a year and half ago. Everybody's hanging at the Escort these days."

"Where's that?"

He gave her the location and she was left confused. "Didn't that used to be a dry cleaners?"

"Yeah. In fact, Brick, the man that owned the cleaners owns the club. He figured that was a better moneymaker."

Crystal shook her head in confusion. Who turned a dry cleaners into a dance club? "So, are you and Unique going there tonight?"

He blasted that smile again. "I think that can be arranged. You got a phone? I'll give you my number."

She fished it out of her backpack.

"Whoa. You really have moved up in the world. That's top of the line. And so is that leather jacket you're wearing."

"Yeah," was all she said, figuring the less attention she gave the remark the better. She slid the phone open and saw what appeared to be a hundred missed calls and texts from her mom. Guilt spread through her like heat. "What's your number?"

He recited while she tapped.

He added, "Give me a call around ten. Gotta be twenty-one to get in though."

"Okay." She tucked the phone away and saw him eyeing her backpack.

"Nice pack."

"Thanks."

"You should let me drive you around and show you some of the changes around here," he offered smoothly. "I'm free for the rest of the day."

"Think I want to check in with Kiki first. How about tomorrow or the day after."

"Sounds good."

He turned the Audi into a large, aging condo complex and wove them around to a row of buildings near the back. "Kiki and Bobby live in that one there."

"Okay, thanks, Ross. I'll give you a call later." She put her hand on the door.

"I don't get a kiss for my trouble."

She grinned. "No, because I don't want trouble from Unique."

"I won't tell if you won't."

"Bye, Ross." Laughing she made her escape.

Watching him drive off, she warned herself to be careful around him. Last thing she needed was drama, especially from Ms. Unique Ralston.

CHAPTER THREE

In response to the bell, the door opened and the sight of her best friend on the other side made Crystal's happiness soar until she heard, "Whatever you're selling, I don't want it."

"Wait!" Crystal cried before the door closed again. "Kiki, It's me! Crystal Chambers."

Kiki slowed and gave her a critical up and down. When the recognition registered, she threw open the door and her arms. "Crystal!"

A hug filled with laughter and rocking followed. Tears stung Crys's eyes.

"Where've you been?" Kiki whispered. "Oh, my god! I've been so worried. Come in. Come in."

Inside, a grinning Crystal stood while Kiki checked her out. "You look good girl! How'd you know I lived here?"

"I ran into Ross."

A baby's cry interrupted the reunion and Kiki instantly turned her head to the sound.

"Ross said you have twins?"

"I do. Come meet your niece and nephew."

Crys followed her through the sparsely furnished apartment and into the kitchen. The sight of two babies seated in matching child chairs put a smile on her face. "They're so cute."

Kiki picked up the crying infant. It quieted and snuggled close. "This, is Bobby Jr. Probably needs his diaper changed. That's my baby girl, Tiara."

The little girl with her curly hair and big black eyes was contentedly gnawing on a small, cloth doll. "They both look just like you and Bobby. Ross said they're almost a year old?"

"Nine months. I love them to death, but these have been the longest nine months of my life. Babies are a lot of work."

Only then did Crystal see the weariness in her friend. There were dark circles under her eyes and her shoulders were slumped. Although she went about the diaper change with a practiced precision, she moved like a woman far older than nineteen. The long black weave she once wore when they ran the streets together was no more. Her real hair was pulled back into a short tail and it was obvious from the dry, rough texture that it hadn't been permed in a while. Crystal glanced around the kitchen, taking note of the old electric stove with its burned black eyes, the old fridge and the small sink filled with a few glasses and bowls. The small dining table and its two chairs appeared to be as old as everything else in the room. The off-white walls were badly in need of paint and the small window over the sink had a cracked pane plainly visible through the clear plastic it was covered by. "How long have you been living here?"

"About six months. We stayed with Bobby's mom after the babies were born. When the state finally came through with the paperwork for subsidized housing, we moved in."

Crystal knew it was wrong but she couldn't help comparing her present surroundings to the bright beautifully furnished house she'd left behind. The calls and messages waiting to be acknowledged on her phone pulled at her, but she was determined not to let them get to her.

"So, where've you been?" Kiki asked.

"Kansas."

"Kansas? Wizard of Oz, Kansas?"

Crystal nodded, and while Kiki fed her kids lunch, she relayed what her life had been about for the past four years

"And this lady adopted you?" Kiki asked skeptically at one point.

"Hard to believe, I know, but, yeah. She's really nice. And she has her own private jet."

Kiki laughed, "You are so lying."

"No, I'm not." Crystal told her about the white jet and pilot Katie Skye. "I've been to Madrid, Barcelona, Paris, Hawaii. Here let me show you some pictures." Once again, she looked past the messages lined up in her inbox and tapped up the photos.

Kiki looked over her shoulder at the picture of Ms. Bernadine. "Wow, love her earrings."

"She real classy."

"Who're those boys?"

"That's Amari, Preston and Devon. We all came to Kansas at the same time."

"Do you get along?"

"Sometimes, but mostly they're a pain in the behind. That's Zoey. She's the little sister of the group."

"She white?"

"Yep and her adopted mom is the old-school singer Roni Moore."

"Estelle has a bunch of her CDs. She lives there too?"

"Yep. Same street."

"Wow."

Looking at the pictures touched Crystal's heart in ways she didn't want to acknowledge.

Kiki retook her seat and asked, "What about your real mom? You ever find her?"

Crys slowly swiped the phone closed and thought back on those memories. "Yeah. She was in jail up in Illinois. When I got to see her she didn't even know who I was."

Kiki stopped in the midst of feeding Tiara. "I'm sorry, Crys."

She shrugged. "I'm good. Finally getting to see her was the most important thing. She died a few months later from HIV."

"Damn."

"Yeah," Crystal responded softly.

"So, it's been awesome and sad all at the same time."

"More awesome but yeah, sad too. And my dad showed up about a year after that."

"Your dad? What the hell did he want?"

"Money. Kidnapped me and held me for ransom."

"Did your mother pay up?"

"She didn't have to. He and I got caught in a tornado. I wound up in Intensive Care. He wound up dead on top of a picket fence. Served him right."

Kiki shook her head as if finding the tale unbelievable. "This sounds like a book."

"I know."

Lunch ended with Kiki wiping the babies' faces and cleaning up the trays on their chairs. After placing the bowls in the sink, she gave Tiara back her doll, handed Little Bobby a cloth truck and joined Crystal at the table. Once again, Crystal noted her over all tiredness. She really wanted Kiki to smile and joke like she used to, but didn't know how to make that come about. "When was the last time you got a good night's sleep?"

"Nine months ago," she said with a weary smile. "Taking care of them and trying to be there for Bobby doesn't leave much room for anything else."

"How're you two doing?"

"Good, but he's stressing from working two jobs and doing his GED on the weekends. He's the hardest working man in Texas."

"I stopped by your mom's place first. She said she put you out and didn't know where you were."

Kiki blew out a breath. "And doesn't care apparently. Right after I told her I was pregnant, she kicked me out. Said I had no respect for her or myself. Dogged out Bobby. I was glad to leave to tell you the truth. Haven't talked to her since she came to visit me at the hospital after I had the babies. Bobby's mom stepped right up, though. Told me I could stay with her as long as I needed."

"That was nice."

"Yeah. She's always been nicer to me than Estelle ever was to Bobby. She helped me a lot during the pregnancy. She hoped the babies would make Bobby grow up."

"Did they?"

"Oh yes. The day after the twins were born he walked away from all the shit he'd been doing in the streets and got a job. And when it wasn't enough to pay the bills he got another. Now, he's working two."

Crystal thought back on Ross's dismissive remarks and how clueless that made him seem. "Where's he working?"

"Valet crew at a car dealership during the week and parks cars for a hotel downtown Friday and Saturday nights. Saturday mornings he's in school."

"You sound proud of him."

"I am. He wants the twins to have all the things we never had growing up. I'm hoping once they're old enough to go to Head Start, I can start doing hair again and bring in some cash. He's all about making our life better and I'm right there with him. And who knows, I may even go get my GED. Did you finish school?"

Crystal wasn't ready to confess the truth about turning her back on school, so she replied vaguely, "I'm almost done."

"Good. Books equal bucks, as Bobby keeps saying."

Crystal changed the subject. "Ross said he's with

Unique Ralston now. What's up with that?'

Kiki shook her head with disgust. "I can't stand her. Never could. Right after you fell off the set, I guess she didn't want to be Miss Moneybags anymore. No idea what the details were but she suddenly showed up with Ross. Didn't graduate, didn't go to college, gave her mom and dad fits from what I heard. Still thinks she's better than everybody though."

"Ross said they'd take me to the club tonight. You and Bobby want to go?"

"Do I look like I have time for clubbing?"

"I thought maybe you'd get a babysitter and then – "

"Sitters cost money. All the money we have goes for diapers, bills and food. Besides, hanging out doesn't do it for us anymore, especially if we have to be with Ross and Unique."

Crys wasn't sure what to make of this new Kiki.

"And truthfully, Unique's not going to want you even looking at Ross, let alone accepting his invitations. Everybody knows how he is, and so does she."

"I don't want her man."

"Doesn't matter. In her world, everybody wants Ross, and it's her job to play pit-bull. She's going to take one look at you in your fine clothes and off the hook hair and want to fight."

"But – "

"But nothing. And you don't need to be hanging with Ross anyway. He's trouble. Always has been."

"Since when did you become so stiff?"

"Since I went through 28 hours of labor and decided I wanted more out of life than Hennessy and being out all night."

"Wow."

"I've grown up, Crys. It happens when life changes

you, and I'm trying to be all over it."

This was definitely not the old Kiki. Crystal had been expecting to hook up with her and pick up right where they'd left off.

Kiki asked, "So how long are you staying in Dallas?"

She shrugged. "Depends on whether I can find a job."

Kiki looked confused. "Why do you need a job. Aren't you just visiting?"

Crystal hesitated, then finally confessed, "No. I'm back here permanently."

"Why?"

She shrugged. "I miss my life here."

"Have you lost your damn mind?'

Crys's lips tightened.

"You have someone footing the bill for what sounds like the perfect life, and you came back here! Did your mom say it was okay?"

When Crystal didn't respond, Kiki eyes widened. "You ran away, didn't you?" She now viewed Crystal as if she'd grown an extra head. "How could you throw all that away?"

"I can get it back on my own. I'm just tired of being cooped up in Nowhere Ville. You don't know what it's like."

"You're right. I got no clue how it feels to have somebody take me in, give me a big pretty room, fly my ass around on a jet and pay for me to go to college. I'd definitely prefer living on food stamps, with two babies, and no life."

Crys was mad.

"I love you, Crys and I'm so glad to see you, but you're not thinking here."

Crys stood up. If Kiki didn't understand, screw it. She'd find someplace else to go.

Kiki snapped, "What? You're going to walk out now, and go where? Sit your dumb behind down."

An angry Crystal sat. Alma the truck driver came off

like Tamar. Kiki was doing a damned good imitation of Ms. Bernadine's assistant Lily Fontaine July.

"I'll let you stay here for three days, then you need to take yourself back home. There's nothing for you here, Crys. Nothing but drama and trouble."

"Three days should be plenty of time to find a job. I'm not going back. I'll be fine. You'll see."

"And you're not seeing how blessed you are, girl."

Crystal's sullen side continued to rule. Parts of her agreed with Kiki – she had left behind a blessed life, but the stubborn parts dug in its heels and wanted to tell Kiki to mind her own damn business. "I have some money. I can pay you for putting me up."

"You're the closest thing I've ever had to a sister. I'm not taking money from you." Her tone then mellowed. "We were a good team back in the day though, weren't we?"

Their old bonds surfaced and Crys nodded. "Remember the time your mom went to Georgia to visit your aunt and we had that house party?"

Kiki laughed. "And she came back a day early? I can still hear her screaming at us."

For the next little while they watched the babies and reminisced.

"Whatever happened to Toni Greer?" Crys asked. "Is she still singing?" Toni had been a member of their crew and blessed with a voice that rivalled Mariah's. Everyone knew she was destined for stardom.

"Two kids by two different guys. She and I share a worker so I see her every now and then. Last time I talked to her she was bragging about a new man. Hope she'll make him wrap it up. She needs zero more babies."

Crystal found that disappointing. "How about Tink?"

"Now, Tink has it going on. Joined the Air Force a year and a half ago."

"You're kidding?" Tink's real name was Deirdre. In the fifth grade, she was dubbed Tink because everything she owned from her backpack to her socks sported Disney's Tinker bell.

"She and I stay in touch. She's in Japan right now, but she's sent me postcards from Germany, Hawaii, Guam. She signed up right before I got pregnant. She tried to get me to go in with her, but …." Kiki 's voice trailed off.

"Why didn't you go?"

"I thought it was a stupid idea." But the way she stared off at something only she could see Crystal wondered if she might be regretting the stance. "My life would certainly be different, that's for sure, but I wouldn't give up my babies for anything in this world." As she viewed her twins, love shone in her eyes.

"And Lisa?" Crys asked. "What's she up to these days."

Kiki's face clouded. "Lisa's dead. Boyfriend shot and killed her last summer. The funeral was so sad. Her mother was a wreck, so was I. He's on Death Row."

Crystal sighed. She thought back on how tight the five of them had been four years ago, and how only she and Tink seemed to have come to the present unscathed. It was sobering.

While Kiki put the twins down for their nap, Crystal sat on the black faux leather sofa that would double as her bed and took out her phone. Thoughts of Lisa haunted her. In the years Crystal spent living in Dallas, she'd known several people whose lives were cut short by violence, but never anyone close to her heart. All the messages and texts from her mom stared up at her accusingly. Among them were other numbers she recognized as belonging to Eli, Preston, and Amari. She wanted to continue ignoring them, but couldn't, so she replied to her mom: *I'm ok. Don't worry.*

There was an immediate response. *Worried. Please call so we can talk. I love you!!!*

Crystal closed the phone.

CHAPTER FOUR

After the twins' nap, it was time for Kiki and the babies to pick Bobby up from work. "Do you want to go with us or hang here?" Kiki asked.

"I'll go."

With Crystal carrying Tiara and Kiki carrying Little Bobby, they walked to an old beat up grey van parked a few feet away. Crystal watched and waited while Kiki went through the elaborate ritual of putting the children in their matching car seats.

With the kids secured, Crys rode shotgun while Kiki steered the noisy clunker out of the complex and onto the city streets. As they drove Crystal checked out the neighborhood. Four years ago, she'd know the area so well she could've found her way through the streets blindfolded and in the dark. Now? "Lots of things have changed," she said, noting a former gas station that was now a no name dollar store.

"The landmarks yes, but not the crime. Estelle got robbed so many times she closed the shop."

Crystal had never like Estelle but was sorry to hear she'd had to close her beauty shop. Kiki had just began working there after school and weekends when Crystal left Dallas.

The drive took them past their old elementary school. The kids were getting out for the day and Crystal noted their young innocent faces. "Did we look like them, back in the day," she asked as the van waited at a red light so the children could cross the street.

"I guess so. They look like babies, don't they?"

Crystal wondered what their dreams were and if they'd be cut short by violence, early pregnancies or homelessness. She also wondered how many of them would opt to find life elsewhere like Tink. And what of her own dreams, she asked herself. For the past few years she'd had her heart set on becoming a world class artist. Would that be possible now that she was on her own? She thought about her unfinished triptych and the contest. Would Ms. Bernadine finally get fed up with her not returning home and toss the canvases in the garbage? Unable to answer the questions, she stared unseeing out her window.

The van pulled away from the light and after a few minutes Kiki turned down a side street.

"Hey stop!" Crystal called out urgently. The familiar house on the corner brought back another round of memories. "Does she still live here?"

"Far as I know," Kiki answered quietly.

"Do you mind if I run in for a minute?"

"No, but try and make it quick, okay. I don't want to be late."

Uneasy about how this might go and even more uncertain about what she might say, Crystal climbed the steps and rang the bell.

When the door opened Mrs. Verna Wagner peered out. "May I help you, honey?"

"Hi, Ms. Verna. It's me, Crystal."

Like everyone else Crystal had encountered that day, the elderly woman puzzled over that pronouncement, then, finally asked, "My Crystal?"

"Yes, ma'am."

"Oh, my lord!" The door opened and Crystal was

pulled into a tight hug that brought tears. "Oh, my goodness," Mrs. Wagner gasped. "So good to see you. So good." Aided by her cane, she stepped back on legs swollen from diabetes and viewed Crystal again. "Look at you," she said emotionally. "Come in."

Mrs. Wagner wiped at her tears while Crystal did the same. "I can't stay but a minute."

"That's okay."

Inside Crys was immediately assaulted by the combined scents of liniment and mothballs. During the five years she'd lived there, she'd hated the smell because it permeated her bedding and clothing thus making her the target of ridicule and snickering at school. The furniture in the pink walled living room hadn't changed. The big green sofa and matching chairs were still pristine beneath the thick sheets of transparent plastic.

"Sit, sit," Ms. Wagner indicated encouragingly.

On the mantle above the fireplace stood framed pictures of her two adopted sons, Marlon and Keith. "How are the boys?" Crystal asked. She really hoped they'd hadn't met tragic ends.

"Doing just fine. Marlon is an EMT down in Houston and Keith is on the police force here. Married nice young women and gave me five good looking grandkids."

Silence crept between them and Crystal mentally searched for words to explain her actions of four years ago. "I just wanted to stop by and apologize for running off the way I did."

"You worried me. I thought maybe you'd been killed or something. I went to the police but they couldn't help."

"I know. I'm sorry." And she was. The retired nurse had taken her in as a nine-year-old foster child and given her a home; the nicest one she'd lived in up until that point, however, she never appreciated it because it felt like just another stop in a long line of places where she never belonged.

"What's it been now, four, five years since I saw you last?"

"Yes, ma'am."

"You look well, so life must be treating you okay."

When Crystal didn't respond, Verna peered at her face and asked knowingly, "Still restless, are you?"

Crystal thought that a good word to describe her feelings. "I think so, yes."

"You always were. Even when you were little you could never sit still. Not even at the dinner table. I'd come home after working the night shift and find you sitting in the living room watching the TV. I don't ever remember you sleeping all night. It was like something was keeping you from settling in."

Crystal nodded at the memory.

"We all have to settle in sometime somewhere, honey," she said and her eyes radiated such profound sadness Crystal had to look elsewhere.

"Did you run because of something I did, or said?"

"No, ma'am."

"Was it the boys?"

Crystal shook her head. "It was just me being restless like you said, I guess."

"You ever find your mother?"

"Yes."

"Did it work out like you imagined?"

"No," she whispered.

"Life is that way sometimes – really most of the time."

Crystal was starting to see that. The debacle with Diego July came to mind. That hadn't worked out as she'd hoped either.

"You want some advice from an old lady way past her

prime?"

Crystal smiled a little. "Yes."

"Stop running. Plant your feet in whatever soil will make you grow, and let the sun shine on your face so you can bloom the way the Good Lord intended you to."

Crystal thought about Henry Adams and Ms. Bernadine.

"Or you can spend the rest of your life chasing after something that will always be just beyond your fingertips."

A car horn sounded. Kiki. "That's my ride," she said quietly. "I have to go."

"I understand."

Crystal stood. "It was nice seeing you."

"Same here."

Mrs. Wagner struggled up and slowly walked her back to the front door. "Take care of yourself, Crystal."

"I will. Tell the boys I said, hey."

"Will do."

"How'd it go?" Kiki asked as she pulled away from the curb.

Crystal shrugged. "Okay, I guess."

"You want to talk about it?"

She shook her head. "No."

Kiki watched her for a moment, then nodded understandingly. "Okay, then let's go get Bobby."

On the ride there, Crystal was lost in thought. Ms. Verna had probably gone out of her mind with worry the night Crystal hadn't come home, and she wondered how long it had taken her to resign herself to the reality that her foster child was gone for good. And now, she was on that same path, but with Ms. Bernadine left to wonder and worry. Crystal left Henry Adams last night with a clear plan on what she wanted and how to obtain it, but once again things weren't going as expected. Mrs. Wagner had given a name to what Crystal had been feeling inside for the past few weeks. Restlessness. *Or you can spend the rest of your life chasing after something that will always be just beyond your fingertips.* So, what am I chasing, she asked herself. Initially it had centered on the freedom to come and go as she chose. Now, she wasn't so sure.

Kiki pulled into the lot of a small used car dealership. Upon seeing all the shiny vehicles Crystal found herself thinking about the car she'd been promised upon graduation. "What exactly does Bobby do here?" she asked to distract herself from yet another blessing she'd turned her back on.

"He cleans the cars, vacuums the interior and washes and waxes the exterior. Sometimes he sweeps the floors. Mows the grass. Whatever he's asked to do basically. He's hoping to find a connect to learn detailing. You know that show - Pimp My Ride?"

Crystal did. Amari watched it all the time.

"He wants to own a shop like that. He's hoping once he gets his GED, someone will take him on. You know like an apprentice." She found a place to park the van and cut the ignition. "Time for you to get in the back with the kids. He'll be coming out in a minute."

Crystal got out and opened the back door. The twins who'd been babbling away during the ride, suddenly quieted and eyed her.

Kiki turned around in the seat. "Make room for Auntie Crystal back there you two."

When Bobby walked up, Kiki got out and gave him a kiss. "Hey baby. How was your day?"

He shrugged. "Same grind. Different day. How was yours?" He was dressed in a blue, short sleeved, buttoned downed shirt with the logo of the dealership on the front pocket. His extensive tats curled up his arms and peeked out above the neck of his shirt.

"Twins didn't run me too ragged, and we have a visitor."

"Who?"

"She's in the back with the kids."

He stuck his head inside the van's open door and the kids babbled with excitement. "Hey you two. You been good?" He placed a kiss on each small forehead and upon seeing Crystal, paused.

"Hi Bobby. Been a minute."

He cocked his head, stared at her for a moment then looked back at the smiling Kiki.

'Don't recognize her, do you?" she asked. "At first, neither did I."

He studied Cry's face again. "Sorry for not knowing who you are."

"I'm Crystal. Fathead."

His eyes widened. "Crystal? Goldilocks?" He checked her out again. "The three bears steal your hair?" He ran around to her side of the van and hugged her. "Wow, look at you looking all prosperous, as my grandma used to say. How you been? Where you been?"

"Semi long story. Been in Kansas, but now I'm back." Crys ignored Kiki's silent show of disapproval.

"How'd you end up there?"

Kiki interrupted. "Let's get home before the babies start fussing. You know they can only stand those seats for so long."

"Okay. You're right." He slid beneath the wheel and turned the key. The van fired up with much rattling and noise from its aged muffler. Bobby nodded a goodbye to one of the other employees and drove off the lot for home. "So, Crys, you here visiting or what?"

"Might be back permanently, if I can find a job."

"How'd you end up in Kansas?"

She began her tale with the night she'd been hitchhiking in the rain and was picked up by a woman who turned out to be a social worker. "She got in touch with Ms. Bernadine who came down to get me."

"In a jet," Kiki tossed in.

"A jet?"

"Tell him how good this lady has been to you Crystal, and that you've been all over the world."

Bobby was studying her via the rear-view mirror and he looked very confused. "You and the lady have a falling out?"

Kiki didn't wait for Crystal to explain. "Nope. She just up and left. Said she felt boxed in."

That seemed to confuse him even more.

Kiki kept going. "Ms. Brown was even going to pay for her college."

"Wow," he uttered softly. "Things must've been awfully bad for you to walk away from all that."

"I told her she was crazy," Kiki summed up.

Crystal snarled. "I was going crazy. There are no clubs, nothing on the radio, they don't even have a McDonald's!"

Bobby looked floored. "I can't believe you left all that just because there was no Mickey Ds."

"It wasn't just about the burgers. It was a lot of stuff."

"Like what?"

"It's hard to explain."

"Leaving all that is crazy, girl."

Kiki chimed in. "I tried to tell her."

"Will you shut the hell up."

"Watch your mouth. There're babies back there, girl."

Crystal was sorry about that but not about the rise in her temper. "If you'd get off me, I wouldn't have to."

"If you had some sense I wouldn't be on you."

"Ladies! Chill. I didn't come home to play referee."

"You're not my mama, Kiki," Crystal pointed out.

"No. Your mama's in Kansas. Probably with a broken heart. Ever think about that!"

Bobby snapped. "Ki, leave her alone."

Kiki huffed back against her seat.

Crystal stared mutinously out her window. No, her return to Dallas was not going well.

CHAPTER FIVE

When they returned to the apartment, vestiges of the tension between the two old friends remained but both seemed willing to look past it. Crystal offered to help with dinner and Kiki graciously accepted. During their years of friendship, Kiki had been the level headed one and Crys the one who hated being told what to do even when Kiki's advice or assessment turned out to be correct. Crystal didn't believe she was right this instance but saw no point in prolonging the argument.

Kiki had always been a great cook, and although the meal was a simple meat loaf, baked potatoes and broccoli, it tasted great. While they ate, Kiki and Bobby caught each other up on their day. Crystal eyed Bobby. He'd grown up in foster care, too and his dark skin was reminiscent of the Julys. Although the former gang member wasn't very tall he was muscular. Back home in Henry Adams his extensive tats would probably draw a lot of stares.

He looked her way. "So, Crys. Where you going to look for a job?"

She thought about the issues surrounding her hunt. "Restaurant maybe. I have some waitressing experience."

He chuckled. "Not only do you look different; you sound different too. That high-class life is rubbing off."

She rolled her eyes but didn't take offense. She agreed

with his take on her outward appearance but disagreed on her speech. "I think I sound the same."

Kiki paused while feeding the twins in their high chairs.

"You don't. Your voice is way more proper. Believe me."

After dinner, Crystal helped Kiki with the cleanup while Bobby took the kids for a walk in the stroller to tire them out before bed.

"So, do you need something to wear to the club?"

"Yeah, I do."

"I got some clothes I'll probably never wear again, so you may as well borrow them."

In the bedroom, she opened the closet and after moving hangers around handed Crystal a pair of chocolate brown leather pants that went nicely with her boots. "I bought them right before I found out I was pregnant."

Crystal planned to pair the pants with one of the cute black tops, she had in her backpack. She and Kiki had always shared clothes, so she knew the pants would probably fit. "Thanks, Ki."

"You're welcome. Just don't get drunk and throw up all over my stuff. You never could hold your cognac."

"I'm gonna overlook that crack."

"Am I lying?"

Laughing, they shared a hug. "Thank you," Crystal whispered.

"No problem. Have fun but when Ross gets here, you'll have to meet him outside. He's not allowed in the house."

"Why not?"

"He and Bobby have been beefing ever since Ross tried to talk Bobby into swiping a key to the dealership so he could go in after the place closed and steal tools and stuff."

"What?"

"Yeah. That's who you'll be rolling with tonight, so watch your back."

Crystal nodded.

When Bobby returned with the kids, he checked out the way Crys was dressed. "Where you heading, Ms. Kansas."

"Some place called the Escort."

"With who?"

She hesitated for a moment before confessing, "Ross."

He sighed and shook his head. "Kiki tell you he and I are beefing."

She nodded.

"Watch yourself. If you need a ride back, give me a call."

"I will."

He took the kids out of the stroller and carried them into the bedroom. He didn't return.

At ten o' clock, Crystal called Ross, and he told her where to meet him. She gave Kiki a hug and set out. It was a chilly night, and she was glad for the borrowed leather pants and her LA jacket. Kiki had also loaned her a small, black, over the shoulder bag that was just large enough to hold her phone, wallet and a fake ID she hoped no one at the door would scrutinize too closely.

Ross's car was parked outside so she pulled open the rear door and slid in. The interior was thick with the smell of pot. "Hey Ross. Hey Unique."

"Hey Crystal. You ready to party?"

"I am."

Unique's stony face was framed by a honey blonde Beyoncé' weave that looked to weigh a good ten pounds. "Don't think we'll be taking you everywhere we go," she said haughtily and then gave Crystal a critical once over. "Where'd you get that coat and those boots."

"Sears," she lied. No way did Unique need to know the provenance of the jacket or the boots.

"I've never seen anything like that in a Sears here. Which Sears?"

Ross groused, "God, 'Nique. Stop sweating her. This ain't Project Runway."

Unique huffed back around in her seat.

Ross headed the car away from the complex and asked Crystal, "You want to hit the blunt?'

"Uh, no. I'm good." Crystal hadn't been around pot since leaving Dallas and although she'd enjoyed taking a hit or two back then, something made her decline. The Kansas part of herself knew the answer: marijuana was an illegal drug and she had no business messing with it, but again, she pushed that logical voice to the side and sat silent while Unique took in a deep draw and exhaled.

Ross asked, "You sure?"

"Yep."

Unique blew out more smoke. "Ross said you were in Kansas City. What's it like there."

"Nice actually."

"When did you start talking like a white girl?"

"When the hell did you start caring what I sound like?" she shot back. Kansas or not, she wasn't putting up with any crap from a Beyoncé wanna be.

Ross shot Crystal a grin in the rear-view mirror but Unique had nothing else to say for the rest of the ride, and Crystal was okay with that.

The small parking lot was full. The former dry cleaner nestled between a Chinese takeout place and an empty building that once housed the neighborhood Kmart, had a large sign over the door that read "The Escort." Crystal couldn't believe all the people streaming in. Framed by car headlights were girls tipping on stilettos in butt high skirts.

Others wore equally short skirts and fur tipped boots that seemed more appropriate for Alaska. She stared like a country girl on her first visit to the city at feathers hanging from waist long weaves of every color imaginable. Ross finally found a place to park.

"Is there a cover charge?' she asked.

Unique rolled her eyes. "Of course. Twenty. And Ross and I aren't paying your way so you better have it."

Snarling silently, Crystal asked Ross to turn on the dome light. When he did, she took her wallet out of her borrowed purse and peeled a twenty off the roll. She glanced up to see Ross and Unique eyeing her wallet with great interest. "Is there a problem?" she asked.

Ross shook his head. "Nope. No problem at all."

But the look he shared with the smugly smiling Unique set off alarm bells. She'd been so focused on going out for a good time, she'd forgotten how much money she was carrying. The Crystal of old would never have left Kiki's with so much cash on her person. Once again, life in Kansas had made her forget how to deal, but as they left the car, Crystal made a note to keep an eye on her purse at all times.

To her relief, the guy on the door barely looked at her fake ID. After taking her twenty and stamping the back of her hand, he waved her on. The moment she stepped into the main room she felt the energy. The darkness, the flashing strobes, the heat of too many bodies, the bone rattling thump of the bass all put a huge smile on her face. For the first in four years she felt like her old self. *Finally!* Happy, she followed Ross and Unique through the tightly packed crowd. She ignored the curious stares from some of the girls she passed. In Henry Adams everyone spoke to everyone else, even strangers. Doing that there would make people wonder what was up with her, so she kept her features closed and unreadable.

Ross apparently had some juice because the approaching hostesses gave him a smile - which made Unique glare - and escorted them to one of the few tables in the place. After they took their seats, Ross ordered three shots of Hennessey. "You down with that, Crystal?" he yelled over the music.

"Oh hell, yeah," she replied without hesitation. She was on her own, getting to do what she wanted and Hennessey with some cola was right up her alley.

The placement of the table had them seated right on the edge of the tiny dance floor and she was loving the music. While the hostess crossed the sea of people to take care of their order, Crystal checked out the dancers. It seemed like an eternity since she'd been on the floor and she couldn't wait to get out there, but she'd never seen the dance everyone was doing.

Ross leaned over and shouted again. "Y'all do the Red Nose in Kansas City?"

Her confusion must've have shown on her face.

"Red Nose! Goes with the Red Nose song."

"Oh, yeah. Yeah," she lied, adding, "I had trouble hearing what you were asking over the music."

Unique looked skeptical but Crystal ignored her and watched the dancers. The women were bent at the waist and popping their hips in time with the music while the guys churned against their behinds. The Kansas in her thought it resembled sex but she pushed the thought aside.

As the music morphed into another song, Unique grabbed Ross's hand. "C'mon Ross. Let's dance. Crystal, pay for the drinks."

Before Crys could protest, they joined the people on the floor. At first, she was upset, but she let it go. They'd been nice enough to let her tag along, the least she could do was pay for the first round.

The Red Nose appeared to be the dance of choice. Some of the guys were grinding against the women so tough they were visibly aroused. She chose to look elsewhere to keep from staring bug eyed.

"Well, hello little mama. Never seen you here before."

Crys turned and looked up into the smiling face of a well - dressed man old enough to be the grandfather of everyone in the place. Gold front teeth flashed in the strobes. "Hi," she said dismissively and resumed viewing the dancers.

"What's your name?" His accent was foreign. African maybe? She wasn't sure.

"Chantelle," she lied.

"Pretty name for a pretty girl. I'm Bricks. I own the club."

"Nice to meet you."

"You live around here?'

"No."

"Don't let my age fool you. I can rock your world, little mama. Got plenty of cash, too. Saw you come in with Ross."

She gave him a distracted nod all the while hoping he'd beat it. The last thing she needed was being hit on by somebody from an old folks' home. The return of the waitress with the drinks was a welcome interruption.

"That'll be thirty-six," the girl announced, setting the glasses down.

"Dollars?" Crystal croaked. When had Hennessy become so pricey?

"Yeah," she replied, giving Crystal a look.

Bricks, told the hostess. "It's on the house."

Crystal was already pulling out two twenties, however. "Thanks, but not necessary. I got it. Keep the change."

The waitress took the bills and disappeared.

"I like a woman who can pay her way."

Crystal sipped her drink and prayed he'd leave.

"Look," he said to her, "I have some business to take care of, but I'm having a private set after the place closes. Consider yourself invited."

"Okay, thanks," she said non - committal like.

He flashed a gold toothed grin and departed.

"Thank you," she gushed aloud, and took a sip from her drink. The liquor instantly warmed her insides, and as it flowed into her blood, she smiled. This is what life was supposed to be about - freedom to do things her way and on her own terms. Feeling good, she raised her glass in a mock toast and declared, "To Henry Adams. Been nice knowing you."

For the rest of the night, she Red Nosed with various guys (even though the grinding made her terribly uncomfortable), drank cognac and generally had the best time in years. On a trip to the ladies room with Unique, the subject of her boots came up again. "Those suede boots are sick. What size do you wear? Let me try them on."

They were standing at the mirror. The room was crowded with so many women wearing so many different styles and colors it was like being in the bird house at the zoo. Pretending not to hear Unique's question Crystal gave her hair and face a quick check and.

"So, what? You ignoring me?"

"No," Crystal replied and made her way to the exit. On the walk back to the table, she realized her legs were a bit wobbly. She assured herself that she was only buzzed, not drunk. She never remembered getting this way so quickly back in the day, but she hadn't consumed any alcohol since being in Henry Adams, and so chalked it up to that. She made a note to slow her roll on the drinks though. She was going to be in Dallas for good, which meant she had plenty of time to work on rebuilding her alcohol tolerance.

Back at the table, she found Ross sitting with Bricks. Crystal fought to keep her reaction to the older man from showing. Unique had no such qualms though; she was angry and didn't care who knew it.

Ross looked between them and asked above the music. What's up?"

"Nothing." Crystal took her seat.

"Bitch dissed me," Unique railed.

Crystal shook her head and turned her eyes to the dance floor.

Apparently, Ross wasn't in the mood for drama because he turned away from Unique and said to Crystal, "Bricks is having an after set. You down with going?"

No, she wasn't and so feigned an elaborate yawn. "I'll have to pass. It's my first day back and between my flight and everything, I need to head back to Kiki's. Can you drop me off first?"

"I was counting on your company," he replied sounding disappointed.

"I'm sorry. Maybe next time."

"Kiki's is out the way," Ross replied. "How about we hang at the after set for a minute and I'll drop you off after?"

She thought about Bobby's offer to give her a ride back if she needed one, but in checking her watch she guessed he was probably in bed. She didn't have the heart to make him get up, get dressed and drive, so she reluctantly agreed. "Okay, but just for a minute."

Unique scowled. "How about she walk home?"

Ross countered. "How about you cut this middle school shit."

"Why're you taking her side over your woman's?"

"Because my woman wouldn't be acting like she's twelve."

From within her Hennessy induced haze, Crystal

smiled smugly.

A short while later, the club began closing down. The crowd was filing out, and the DJ was packing up his equipment. After all the drinks she'd had, Crystal was what the courts would call *impaired,* but she didn't care. She felt good.

Before Bricks departed to do whatever duties were involved with locking up, he turned to Crystal. "I'm looking forward to hanging with you later."

She gave him a fake smile.

"Let's roll," Ross announced. Unique made a point of linking her arm with his as they left the table and Crystal made a point of putting one foot in front of the other to keep from swaying like a palm tree on a beach in Maui. Despite her focus, she tripped and would have gone down in a heap had Ross not quickly reached out and caught her. Laughing drunkenly at herself she pulled herself together.

"You okay?" he asked his smile making her as woozy as the liquor.

"Yeah. Think I'm a little buzzed."

"I think so too."

Had she been in right mind, she would've kept her mouth shut, but as they stepped out into the starry night, the Hennessy made her say, "You know, you are so fine, I could just eat you up."

Unique went ballistic and Ross had to put her in a bear hug to keep her from attacking. "Calm down!"

She screamed, "You're pushing up on my man right in front of my face? You think I'm blind! I will kill you!"

"Whoa. Whoa. Whoa, baby calm down." Ross said while grinning Crystal's way the entire time.

"Let her go," Crystal said easily. "She probably can't fight any better than she did in the fifth grade. Remember that day on the playground, Unique."

"I'll kick your ass!"

Crystal blew out a breath. "Yeah right."

Unique was all flailing arms and legs.

Ross snapped. "Unique, go to the car."

"I'm going to kill that bitch!"

"Go to the car!"

"No! Let me go. Who does she think she is?"

"She's drunk, 'Nique. She probably won't even remember this the next time we see her. Give her a break. She's celebrating.

"That don't include my man!"

"Go. To. The. Car. I'm not going to tell you again."

She was still spitting mad, but finally, after giving Crystal and Ross glares that should've melted them on the spot, she stomped off.

In the silence that followed Crystal liked the way the moonlight played over his fine brown features.

"You want to eat me up, huh?"

"Yeah. Can't wait until I get my own place."

"You're serious, aren't you?"

"As a heart attack, but I don't like to share so you'll have to get rid of the witch."

"I'll keep that in mind."

Flush with victory, she walked with him to the car.

CHAPTER SIX

While Ross drove through the deserted streets to Brick's after-set, the drunk Crystal was glad she'd worn her jacket. Due to the huge drop in the temperature, the interior was cold and she prayed the car's heat would reach her soon. The chilly air had sobered her somewhat, but between the long day and the liquor she was having trouble staying awake. She wanted to go to bed, but truthfully, wasn't looking forward to sleeping on Kiki's cracked fake leather couch because she knew it couldn't compare with her big roomy bed back home with its soft sheets, cozy blankets and comforters. She reminded herself that she'd given up that luxury along with everything else she'd held dear for the past four years by running away. The reality left her a bit melancholy, and as much as she tried not to think about the place she'd called home, its essence pulled at her, bringing back the faces of Ms. Bernadine, Zoey, Eli, and Amari; the sounds of the music on the fancy red juke box at the Dog where she'd worked; and the triptych waiting to be finished. All she'd seen and done with her adopted mom and the people of Henry Adams merged with the advice given to her by her birth mom, Nikki before she died in prison from HIV. "*.... concentrate on getting an education. Go to college ...*"

To her relief, the memories faded as the car slowed and Ross parked, but seeing where they were gave her pause.

"This is where he's throwing the set?" she asked skeptically. Back in the day the building had been the proverbial No Tell Motel with a clientele that made its living doing drug deals and Johns. She and Kiki had gone to a couple of parties inside the cockroach and rat infested place, but never stayed long due to the dangerous crowd and atmosphere.

Ross turned off the ignition and answered her question. "Yeah. He just bought the place. He's planning on rehabbing it into condos."

She peered out at the building's windows. A couple at ground level were lit from within, but the rest were dark and covered with plywood. "Is it abandoned?"

"Pretty much, but he sleeps here sometimes because it's close to the club."

"And it's free," Unique tossed out, speaking for the first time since their earlier altercation. "Brick's cheap. He keeps saying he has all this money. I think he's lying."

"Just get out the car," Ross snapped.

***

There was a small group of people already inside the basement apartment when they entered. Brick threw her a wink that she pretended not to see. Music was thumping and everyone was standing because there was no furniture. The air was pungent with the smell of burning bud that filled the room with a thin smoky haze. As she followed Ross and Unique to a spot near the back wall, she recognized a few faces from the club but no one offered a nod of greeting.

"Here." Unique handed her a lit blunt and a look that dared her to refuse. Rather than be called out, Crystal took a hit and passed it back. A few puffs later her world turned cottony and she swore she was floating. Couples were red nosing to the music while others slipped into what she assumed was the bedroom for reasons she didn't want to think about. But none of it mattered - not the music, or the high-pitched laugher, or whatever Brick was trying to run on her when he came and stood by her side. Because of the blunt, all she could do was stand and smile. Eventually though, the high from the weed combined with the excessive cognac took its toll. She figured if she just sat down for a moment she'd be okay. Once seated on the dirty beige carpet, she leaned her spinning head back against the wall.

It was the last thing she remembered.

***

She awakened the following morning bleary eyed and disoriented. Her pounding head interfered with her thinking so much it took her a moment to realize she was lying face down on a nasty smelling carpet. She dragged herself up to a sitting position hoping that might help her aching head. It didn't. Hunched over she closed her eyes. Memories returned of all the Hennessy and she groaned. She vaguely remembered Ross and Unique helping her to a bathroom. She'd been so messed up. That thought froze her. She sat straight up and looked around. The emptiness of her surroundings echoed eerily. *Where is everybody?* It was if her body had been waiting for her to become lucid enough to remind her of all the liquor she'd consumed. Two seconds later, her stomach roiled ominously. Throwing a hand over her mouth, she forced herself to her feet and quickly stumbled to the bathroom.

When she was done, she felt like she'd run been over by a DART bus. Her mind wanted to explore the mystery of why she was in the apartment alone but her body just wanted to die. Panting and bent over, it came to her that there might be some Advil or something similar in her borrowed purse, so she staggered out of the tiny bathroom to see. But there was no purse lying on the floor where she'd slept. Her leather jacket had disappeared too. Fighting panic, she took a frantic look around then her eyes widened as she saw her bare feet.

"Oh, no!" She tried to force her mind to remember last night's details. When had she taken then off? Had she given her things to someone for safe keeping?

Then, Brick walked in. "What the hell you still doing here?"

"Do you know where my stuff is?" Her head continued to pound.

"What stuff?"

"My purse. My jacket. My boots." *Her phone!*

He glanced down at her feet and laughed. "No."

She thought she might be sick again.

He sidled close enough for her to smell his stale cologne. "Looks like you got a problem little mama, but Bricksy can fulfill all your needs."

"Can I use your phone?" she gritted out. She needed to call Ross.

"Sure. Comes with a price, though." And he slid a bent finger down her cheek.

She slapped his hand away.

The gold tooth gleamed. "Suit yourself."

Fueled by anger and despair Crystal ran past him, ignoring the sound of his mocking laughter.

Outside, a cold gusty wind, coupled with freezing rain stopped her in her tracks, and added to her already awful day. Ross and Unique lived a short distance away from Kiki, so all she had to do was get to Kiki's house and borrow her phone to give them a call. But Kiki lived at least two miles from Brick's building. The thought of having to walk all that way without shoes and a coat made her want to cry, but she had no choice and took off at a run.

By the time she'd covered the first two blocks her clothing was soaked through and her extremities were so numb she was reduced to walking. Having spent winters in Kansas she knew how easy it was to contract frostbite, and she and her bare feet were prime candidates.

The sleet filled rain was torture as she covered another six blocks then ten. Attempting to avoid the frigid puddles and the icy, ankle deep water hugging the curbs as she crossed streets was impossible so she stopped trying. When a DART roared by, she wasn't quick enough to get out of the way and was doused by a wave as large as any she'd seen on Maui. Screaming her anger and frustration she wanted to give up, but trudged on and let the rain mask her tears.

Halfway to Kiki's place a car slid up to the curb and slowed. She didn't recognize the man behind the wheel so she didn't acknowledge him.

He drove beside her slowly and the passenger's window slid down. "You look like you could use a ride, baby girl, and I'm just the man for the job."

After all she'd endured the offer was tempting but she had no idea what might happen once she got in his car. "No thank you!"

"Freeze then, bitch." He roared off.

Exhausted, soaked to the skin, and colder than she'd ever been in her life, she struggled on. Were she back in Kansas, she'd be in the warm confines of her cozy bedroom looking out at the weather, instead of being in it. *This is your own damn fault,* she chastised herself and because it was true she forced herself to keep moving on legs and feet that were stiff and unfeeling as stone.

She finally made it to Kiki's and hit the bell. Kiki took one look at Crystal and instantly cried, "Oh my lord, girl!"

A sobbing Crystal fell into her arms.

"Come, lie on the couch. What happened?"

Aided by her friend, Crystal somehow managed to reach the old couch. While Crystal shivered uncontrollably, Kiki ran to the bedroom and came back with a towel, a robe, the comforter from her bed and a pair of thick socks." Here,

Kiki stilled. "You sure?"

She nodded.

Kiki came around the table and gave Crystal a hug filled with such love and caring, Crys fought off tears. "You made a good decision," Kiki whispered.

After dinner, they got into the tired old van and made their way to the closest precinct. Dressed in a borrowed hoodie and wearing a pair of mismatched fuzzy socks on her feet, she shared a parting hug with Kiki. Both had tears in their eyes.

"Call me when you get home so Bobby and I'll know you're okay."

"I will. Thanks so much for everything."

"You're welcome. Now go and be that new Crystal. She's going to have an awesome life. I can feel it."

"I want you and Bobby to come visit."

"Soon as we save up the money, we will. Promise."

They both knew the chances of that was slim, but neither spoke to that. Instead, they shared another hug and more tears. "Love you, Kiki."

"Love you more, Crys. Now go in before Bobby starts boo-hooing, too."

Crys walked around to where he sat behind the steering wheel and gave him a kiss on the cheek. "Thanks, Bobby."

"Take care of yourself, Goldilocks."

Standing in front of the precinct doors, Crystal watched as they drove away and thought they deserved an awesome life as well. Once the van was out of sight, she wiped her eyes, pulled herself together and went in.

"Can I help you?" asked the lady officer behind the desk.

"Yes. I'm a runaway. I'd like to call my mom."

The woman nodded approvingly. Take a seat on that

get those wet things off and wrap up."

Crystal frozen fingers wouldn't work so Kiki had to help. Once she was in the robe, Kiki's attempts to put the socks on her feet made Crys cry out with pain.

"Your feet feel like ice. Can you walk?"

"Not yet. Give me a minute." She tried to draw in a few calming breaths. She was so cold. "Glad you were home," she whispered from between chattering teeth.

"Me, too. Bobby's mama took the babies for the day. I was just here chilling. Come, need to get you to the kitchen and sit you by the stove. Lean on me."

Crystal's tears flowed unchecked. Every inch of her body ached. The journey to the kitchen seemed to take years, but she finally settled onto a chair and Kiki turned on the oven and opened the door. A few moments later tiny tendrils of heat began wafting over her shaking body. The warmth felt so good Crystal moaned.

"Now what happened? Where's your coat and boots?"

Still shivering beneath the comforter, she answered in a voice hoarsened by the harsh weather, "I don't know. When I woke up, all my things were gone - the purse you let me borrow, my phone, money. Everything."

"Oh, no."

Crystal went on to relate the evening's events as best she could remember, adding, "I shouldn't've gotten so drunk." Embarrassed and feeling stupid, she asked, "Please don't say, 'I told you, so.'"

Kiki shook her head. "I'd never do that. You've been through enough."

Crystal was grateful for the understanding. "I need to call Ross and Unique. Maybe they took my things for safe keeping."

Kiki scoffed, "If Ross and Unique took your stuff it wasn't for safe keeping. This is Ross you're talking about, girl.

"I know, but I'm trying to give him the benefit of the doubt."

"And Unique was grilling you about your boots, too?"

Crystal knew Kiki was right, but refused to relinquish her last frayed thread of hope. "Just call him. Please?"

"Okay. Maybe this'll have a happy ending, even if it is Ross." But when Kiki called, no one answered. She left a message on his voice mail. "What's your phone number? Let's see if it rings."

Crystal gave her the digits, then watched and waited. "Is it ringing?"

She nodded. "No one's picking up though." She let it ring a few more times. Shaking her head with what appeared to be disgust and resignation, she ended the connection.

Crystal couldn't believe this was happening. "That was all the money I had. What am I supposed to do?"

Kiki looked her in the eyes. "You already know, Crys."

Crys turned away. A small part of her wanted to deny reality and say this was just a minor setback and that things weren't as horrible as they seemed, but she knew better. She'd come to Dallas to pick up her old life and instead found disaster. She'd left Henry Adams with such high hopes. Mrs. Wagner's sage words replayed in her head: *Stop running.*

An hour later, Crystal was finally warm enough to almost feel human again. "Hand me your phone. Let me call Ross again."

"He's not going to answer."

Tight lipped she held out her hand. The call went through, but as Kiki predicted, no one answered. She left a message on his voice mail.

Kiki met Crystal's eyes and pointed out softly, "I said I wasn't going to tell you this, but you obviously need to hear it: The old Crystal would never have gotten so drunk she let somebody like Ross take advantage of her."

Crystal's lips thinned.

"You know that's the truth. There's nothing f here anymore. The old life you're chasing after is gon you need to recognize."

But Crystal didn't want to because that meant have to go home to Henry Adams, and the thoug returning with her tail between her legs was wa embarrassing and painful to contemplate. The thoug having to look her adopted mom in the eyes after a worry she'd caused wasn't anything she wante contemplate either. Yet truth be told, she was tired of rur from herself. The pampered, slow living Crystal she'd s all summer complaining about being was obviously wh was now. Kiki was right, she didn't belong here anym Last night's debacle made that crystal clear. She didn't k how she would make it up to Ms. Bernadine but she plan to try real hard – that is if Ms. Bernadine allowed her to c back.

Crystal took a hot shower, careful not to use up much of the house's hot water, then dressed herself in a p of jeans and a top from her backpack. She didn't have anot pair of shoes so she put Kiki's socks back on her still ten feet. When she reentered the kitchen, Bobby was there and t concern in his eyes brought back the pain of her folly. "I' okay," she said softly.

"I can go bust Ross up if you want? Get your thin back."

"And maybe lose your job? No. Nothing's worth a that."

"Sit and have some dinner," Kiki invited quietly "We're going to go pick up the babies in a minute."

"On the way, can you drop me off at the police station? I need to call my mom and see if she'll send me a bus ticket or something so I can go home."

bench over there, honey. Be with you in just a minute."

"Thank you."

While she waited, Mrs. Wagner's words came back to her once more: *Plant your feet in whatever soil will make you grow....*

For Crystal Chambers Brown that soil was in Henry Adams Kansas. If she had her way, Kiki, Bobby, and the twins would be planting their feet in the same soil, too. Soon.

Bonus Short Story - TRANSFORMATION

Note from Beverly Jenkins:

For those of you who don't know, I'm an avid fantasy reader. Authors like N K Jemisin, Ilona Andrews, and Jim Butcher take me on journeys filled with magic, wizards, and dragons. I've always wanted to try my hand at the genre so I've included a very short piece that may or may not grow into something more in the future. I hope you enjoy it.

CHAPTER ONE

Central Africa
1820

Aya loved being human. As a daughter of the Sun and the Moon, she had abilities to take on any form: an eagle in flight, a leopard chasing prey, a honeybee seeking nectar. But by shrouding herself in flesh, she could walk among the people of the villages, relish the warmth of her mother rays, enjoy the kiss of her father's gentle night breezes, and savor the solid strength of Africa's soil beneath her feet. As a human female, she'd witnessed childbirth, learned the art of cooking, planting, and the songs that mourned the dead. As a male, she'd joined the hunts, woven bolts of beautifully colored cloth, and posed as a warrior to a king. Her mother the Sun cautioned her against spending so much time as someone other than herself, but Aya, filled with youthful arrogance and hubris didn't listen.

On the day that would change her life, she learned a local village would be naming its king's infant son. She especially enjoyed celebrations. No matter the occasion, there were always elaborate dishes, skilled musicians, and lots of songs and dancing. As night fell, and her father Moon rose in the sky, torches were lit and the revelry began. Aya had just joined the circle of women for a dance to honor the child's mother when a horde of men brandishing swords and guns rushed into the torch lit village. The king's warriors took up their spears and shields to meet the foe. Chaos ensued. People ran. Women and children screamed. The intruders were slavers; a pestilence that had been scouring the continent for decades. Aya was forbidden to intervene in human affairs, but seeing the newly named baby snatched from his wailing mother, she raised her voice to chant down the whirlwind, only to be felled by a crushing blow to the back of her head.

She was lying on the ground when she regained her senses. The sun was high in the sky. Groggy, head throbbing, she started a chant to return to her true form, but pain doubled her over instead. There was iron encircling her ankles. It was the only man made substance capable of binding a Spirit and it burned like hot coals against her skin. Fear grabbed her. Looking around she saw that she was not alone.

Seated nearby were hundreds of men and women shackled by leg irons and connected to each other by lengths of heavy chain. Slavers stood over them, guns at the ready. Her fear increased. To her shock, shimmering behind the faces of some of the captives were other Spirits of wood, air, fire, and earth who'd apparently been masking as humans, too. Now, like her they were caught and powerless. There were also demon spirits, who though bound, smiled greedily from within their human facades in anticipation of feeding upon the misery and terror. Aya closed her eyes and sent up an urgent plea to her mother for help, but received only silence. She pleaded, begging for forgiveness. Again, nothing. The enormity of her plight was staggering. She had no idea where the slavers were taking them or why. Being immortal and considering herself above the petty worries of humans, it hadn't occurred to her to enquire about the fate of the thousands of Africans taken captive before. Now, she wished she had done so. A short distance away sat scores of chained children. Their anguished cries tore at her heart and she wondered about the fate of the king's son. But it was HER own fate that was most chilling. Until she found a way to be free of the iron, her true self would remain trapped.

She and the other captives were dragged to her feet and forced to march over land to the coast. Some died along the way. Those who balked or could not keep pace were shot.

Weeks later, when they finally arrived, they were fed into the belly of an enormous wooden ship bobbing atop the water like a waiting beast.

CHAPTER TWO

Charleston SC
1820

Ezekiel Grange walked through pens of the city's slave market holding a scented kerchief to his nose against the gagging stench rising from the scores of unwashed African bodies. Having recently inherited a substantial amount of coin from a dead relative, he wanted to buy more slaves to supplement the few he currently owned. Grange was an ambitious man. Through marriage six years ago to the wealthy, buck-toothed spinster Rebecca Ware, he'd advanced from a poor store clerk to a low rung member of Charleston's planter society. In comparison to the truly wealthy, his holdings were small, but his business acumen was sound, and he was convinced it was just a matter of time before his name and estates became synonymous with theirs.

To that end, he'd come to evaluate the blacks for sale. The broadsides circulated upon the arrival of this newly docked slaver claimed it offered an impressive cargo - strong hardy bucks, females ripe for breeding and a number children, which many of his class preferred because they were young enough to be malleable. Once they ceased crying for their mothers and grew older, they'd be docile and content with their lot. As adults, if they were fed and allowed to rest now and again, they'd work from sun up to sun down - much like oxen.

Due to the market's poor lighting, determining which of the captives to place bids upon was difficult, but Grange kept up his slow stroll. Peering back at him out of the gloom were eyes of the furious, the sick, the terrified, and the mad. Having seen enough he left.

Outdoors, the sun was shining. Glad to be free of the stench and gloom, he drew in deep breaths of sweet clean air and walked over to join the other planters to wait for the auctioning to commence.

At first, Aya wondered if this was the Land of the Dead, but seeing no human ancestors, she knew that was not the answer. The ocean crossing had seemed endless. Only occasionally were the captives given precious moments above decks to take in fresh air. Some took advantage of the moments to dive into the sea. As they swam east, many received bullets in their backs but others were left alive so sport could be made while they were eaten by sharks swimming in the ship's wake. Through it all, she continued to plead to her mother for deliverance.

For the moment, she was in a pen filled with women. She didn't know the true numbers of Africans with her but she assumed there were many because the stagnant air was a fetid mixture of sweat, fear, and excrement. Off in the distance the darkness echoed with shrieks of broken minds, wails of the terrified, and low-toned ancestral songs of the dead.

A guard pulled her and a few other women away from the main group and led them away. They were still hobbled so walking was difficult. The line was stopped and they were unceremoniously doused with buckets of cold water which left them gasping and shivering. Afterwards, they were handed thin sack-like shifts to cover their nakedness. To aid the process, their ankle restraints were removed, but her hope that she'd be free of the burning iron long enough to regain her strength were dashed when new shackles were placed on her wrists. She wanted to scream her frustration. Instead she gathered herself and waited for what would follow in this nightmare she'd brought on herself. As the guard roughly prodded them forward, she vowed that when did she escape, she'd never walk the earth as human again.

Grange watched the line of women emerge from the back of the building and saw them instantly draw away from the noon sun as if it brought pain. He assumed it had been some time since they'd stood in full light, but he wasn't concerned with their discomfort. He was in the market for a breeder, maybe two and if he could use one of them to slake his own needs, so much the better. He'd yet to bed an African but he'd heard they were quite insatiable and his groin tightened with anticipation.

The women were now positioned next to the bucks and a small group of children. He shook his head at the haughtiness some of the men and women displayed. It was always a pleasure to watch his overseer break that spirit and show them their rightful place. He focused attention one of the females. She looked particularly angry, and if eyes could kill, not a one of the men who'd come to bid would be alive. He found her tall lean frame to be of interest though.

One by one the Africans were examined. To judge their health, the pen's owner forced their mouths open so Ezekiel and the others could get a good look at their teeth. The Africans strained against their shackles, but the planters ignored it. No one wanted to shell out good coin for a slave already sick from the passage.

The men's genitals were exposed and manipulated to answer questions about each buck's ability to produce seed. The women's shifts were raised to show if their hips were wide enough to bear the number of children necessary to ensure a planter's future. To Ezekiel's trained eyes, the tall lean woman he'd found interesting earlier appeared to be young. With the right mating, she'd likely produce seven, eight - maybe more. He approached her to physically gauge the size and heft of her breasts. At his handling, she didn't flinch or cower. Instead she stared back with the arrogance of a queen. Smiling faintly, he turned away and placed his bid on her.

Minutes later, she and three others - a man, a woman and a girl child were put in the back of his wagon. He climbed onto the seat and signaled his African headman Jeremiah, to guide the team of horses home.

CHAPTER THREE

As the wagon bumped along the uneven tract Aya's fury consumed her. Had she been sold? After being handled like a beast and witnessing all that had transpired back at the pens, the answer could only be yes. Did they not know who she was? Did they not know that the only thing between them and death were the shackles around her ankles and wrists? It was obvious they didn't, and being in no position to illuminate them only increased her rage and underlying misery. Why hadn't her mother answered? Were the irons smothering her appeals? She had no answers. She took a moment to assess the other captives riding with her. The man's eyes blazed with an anger that mirrored her own, the woman too. Tears spilled down the cheeks of the little girl and the woman took her upon her lap and held her close.

Aya was curious about the African holding the reins. Had he been purchased as well? She wanted to ask him how long he'd been in the land, but held onto her questions until she could speak to him alone. The slaver beside him must've sensed her interest because he turned and looked directly at her. She met his knowing smile distantly and focused her attention on the countryside. She already knew what he had in mind, which meant he'd be the first to die.

After some time, the wagon finally came to a halt in front of a large house made of stone and wood. Around it were open fields bordered by trees. In the fields, a group of Africans stopped their digging to watch Aya and the others disembark.

"This is your new home," the African driver said to them in the common language the African tribes shared. "My name is Jeremiah. The white man is Marse Granger. He now owns you."

Aya assessed the white man who now had a name.

"You will work for him until death. If you run away, you'll be found and whipped."

Granger addressed them in words she didn't understand so she paid him no mind and kept her attention focused on Jeremiah who translated, "Marse Granger says if you work hard, you'll be treated fairly."

A man with a gun walked up to join them. He was pale, short and stout. There was a black whip hanging from the belt at his waist and his blue eyes were cold as a demon's. The driver Jeremiah introduced him as Sales. "He's the overseer. He makes sure you put in a good day's work and will punish you if you don't."

Sales said something to Jeremiah. Again, he translated, "He expects to you to be able to understand his words as soon as possible. Doing so will make it easier to know what you're supposed to do in the fields. You'll also be given new names."

And at that moment, the one she knew as Granger pointed her way and said the word, "Sarah." She supposed it was what she was to be called. She saw no harm in answering to it. For now. Eventually, she'd reclaim the name given to her by her mother at her creation. The man Granger gave her a final long look then turned and walked towards the wood and stone house.

Sales then removed their irons. Aya sighed with relief. The burning ceased and a low hum of power entered her body through the land beneath her bare feet. It was very weak however, lacking the the vitality and sacredness that flowed with such force back home. It felt as if its innate power had been fouled somehow. She glanced up and found the driver watching her intently - *he knows,* came the thought. Careful not to stare, she studied him closely while he gave further instructions on what was expected. There was a faint glimmer around his form, as if he were Spirit born too, but the sparks were dim as dying coals.

She and the others were taken by Jeremiah and Sales to a place the called the "quarters," where they would sleep during the hours they weren't toiling. The walls and roof were made of old wood slats, and there was a thin pallet filled with husks to sleep on. She and the woman who'd accompanied her from the pens, now named Ollie, were to share the space.

They were instructed to rest up for the remainder of the day. It was late afternoon, and work would begin at sunrise. The moment the men left, Ollie laid down and cried softly until she drifted off to sleep. Aya didn't need sleep, nor did she need to eat. All she needed was enough power to take on her true form so she could kill the slavers and return home.

CHAPTER FOUR

As dusk arrived, Ollie awakened and left Aya to find food. Moments later, Jeremiah entered. He studied Aya silently for a moment. "Greetings, Spirit."

She inclined her head. "Greetings to you. How long have you been in this place?"

"Ten years."

She sighed with the sadness of that. "Are you content?"

He shook his head. "I was born of the Fire, but his land lacks what I need to break the cage over my true form."

"How were you taken?"

He offered a bittersweet smile. "I was making love to the wife of a king. He discovered us and before I could escape, he pierced my side with an iron spear. The pain left me so weakened, his men had no trouble binding me with chain. I was sold to the slavers the next day. And you?"

She told him her story.

"Sad. Sadder still is there's no way home. The longer you walk this land the weaker you become, until finally you begin aging just as humans do. There's nothing for us to look forward to but death."

The revelation was appalling. There was no such thing as death to an Immortal, yet he was telling her that would be her fate. "I will find a way home."

"At first, I believed that, but now I'm resigned."

"Are there many of us here?"

"No, but we're all destined to spend the rest of their days under the boot and lash of the slavers."

"Do they know of us?"

"No. They consider us dumb beasts, incapable of performing the wonders we once had at our fingertips. Even if they were told, they wouldn't believe. Their knowledge of our world is as limited as their minds."

"Tell me about this place and these people."

She listened to his tales of being forced to work like beasts in the fields, of little food and even less care. Of how those who tried to escape were hunted down by men with dogs, returned, tied to the whipping tree, and whipped until the blood ran down their backs like rivers. Repeat offenders were branded with hot irons, and in extreme cases had feet or legs severed to make them stay enslaved.

Suddenly, Granger was standing in the doorway. He began speaking. Aya didn't understand his words but by the suspiciousness in his eyes, she thought he might be asking Jeremiah his purpose for being there.

Jeremiah replied calmly.

Granger looked between the two of them as if trying to determine the truth in Jeremiah's words. He seemed satisfied but barked two words.

Jeremiah nodded and left them.

Granger then turned his attention her way. Aya didn't

possess the full breadth of power she was accustomed to wielding. This fouled land had so far only supplied her with a small amount, but should he attempt what she saw in his eyes, she'd only need a small amount to make him wish he'd left her at the pens.

Ezekiel smiled at the woman he'd named Sarah. He'd spent all afternoon thinking about the acts he wanted her to perform on him, and now, just the sight of her tall lean frame added to the hard need in his loins. He remembered how hot the skin of her breasts had been in his hands, and he wanted to know if the rest of her held the same heat. "You and I are going to get along very well."

He knew she didn't understand his words, but it didn't matter, she'd understand plenty when he got between her thighs. To that end, he closed the distance between them. He grabbed the neck of her shift and suddenly found himself up by the ceiling of the room! Terrified, eyes wide, he flailed and kicked, but was held there as if by the invisible hand of God. He stared down. She wore a small smile but there was a dark storm roiling in her eyes.

"Stop this!" he demanded.

Instead, she began a sing song chant that raised the hairs on the back of his neck.

"I'll have you whipped to death, you African bitch!"

He was slammed to the earthen floor so forcefully, he cried out in pain, only to be raised high again. Blood poured from his nose. Her smile turned deadly. He hit the ground again with even more force. He screamed and was above her once more. Her dark eyes taunted him. He begged, "Please!"

But there was no mercy. She repeated the witchery.

This time, his ribs and pelvis exploded from the impact. And as he lay there moaning, unable to move, the last thing he remembered before sliding into unconsciousness was her stepping over him as she walked out into the night.

CHAPTER FIVE

Based on what Jeremiah told her of the slavers punishments, Aya was certain she'd be facing death should she be found and returned, but that fate was preferable to a life of servitude and physically servicing Granger. She'd taken such pleasure in introducing him to who and what she was. She'd been careful not to kill him because she wanted him to suffer and for that suffering to linger; hopefully for the rest of his days. He and his kind were plagues on her homeland, and now, she'd taken a modicum of revenge for all the grief and misery they'd caused. But she was no closer to going home. Her appeals to her mother hadn't borne fruit, so the time had come to appeal to her father. She was seated in a small clearing a few miles away from Granger's quarters. Father Moon was high in the sky and she was bathed in the rays of his cool light. She sent up a prayer filled with her despair and longing. She also pleaded for forgiveness, then settled in to wait.

A few moments later, to her surprise and delight, he shimmered into view, cloaked in the form of an African king. She bowed her head. "Father. Thank you coming."

He sat beside her and drew her to his side, then kissed

her brow. "I cannot stay long because other gods rule here, but take this." He handed her a small root. "It's a gift from your Mother. You've been away too long to return to who you were, so you must swallow it. In three days, it will help you transform."

She studied the small brown thing and looked up to question him about it but found herself alone. "Father!"

On the wind, she heard him whisper. "Three days, daughter. Hide yourself away, then return to the slavers. You will need their help."

Return to the slavers? What kind of help could Granger possibly offer? The words made her wary, but had she listened to her mother's advice she wouldn't be enslaved, so she swallowed her misgivings along with the root and tried not to worry.

With the aid of her limited powers she kept herself hidden from the roving groups of men and dogs hunting her by turning herself into small things like tiny birds, fish and honeybees. She couldn't hold the forms for very long but it was enough. Since swallowing the root the area surrounding her spine itched constantly, and her skin felt as if it were drying out and shrinking. Her fingers and toes were becoming misshapen, the nails turning black. *What is happening to me?* Once again, she had questions for which there were no answers, so on the third day, she came out of hiding and walked back to Granger's land.

The first thing Sales the overseer did upon her return was to hit her so hard in the face with his closed fist she fell to the ground. Kicks followed, breaking ribs and filling her with a pain so raw she cried out. Pain was new to her, and now that she'd had her first taste she didn't want more, but knew this was only the beginning. He dragged her to her feet, then across the field to a large tree, all the while screaming at her with such ferocity, his spittle sprayed her face. He forced her arms around the tree and tied her to it using a length of stout hemp around her wrists. Blessedly It wasn't iron but it didn't matter, she had neither power nor strength. The surface of the trunk against her face had no bark and was smooth as glass. It was stained with a red that could only be blood. A whipping tree. How many other captives would've had to stand in this place for their blood to become so embedded. Her knees weakened at the reality of the answer. And where was the transformation her father promised?

But there was no time for further questions. Granger arrived, carried on a litter by Jeremiah and three male slaves. She gloried in the sight of him bandaged from head to feet. The other captives stood gathered a few feet away. She sensed by their sad stoic faces that they weren't there by choice. She was being used as both an example and a warning.

The itch in her back seemed to have caught fire and her spine felt as it were roiling and moving in and out as if taking breaths. Sales grabbed her attention when he moved close and showed her the whip. He growled something and using his hands split the shift covering her back in two. He gasped in shock. Aya cautiously turned her head and saw her spine had developed an enormous hump. To her further surprise the flesh over it was moving as if harboring something alive. Sales eyes grew wide. She saw him hastily glance Granger's way. She again wondered about the nature of the root she'd been given until the lash of the whip flayed her back like a bolt of lightning and it took all she had to keep her screams inside. Again, and again the terrible whip scored her. Closing her eyes, she prayed to every Immortal she knew, but the whip kept falling until her knees sagged and the blood ran down to her hips. Someone was screaming and she realized it was she. In the dizzying haze of the pain she thought she'd gone mad upon hearing a voice in her head, say, *"Hold on, little one. It's almost time."*

"Mother?" her mind whispered back.

"No. I am more."

The crack of the whip became unceasing as did the agony. Sales seemed intent upon whipping her to death and she, who'd long since lost all sense of time and place prayed it would come soon. Then a row of raised scales sharp as African diamonds exploded from her spine. Her body began expanding and the rope on her wrists snapped as her arms elongated, talons the color of obsidian replaced the nails on her hands and feet, and her skin began changing from brown to scales of faceted greens, indigo and blacks. Those gathered around the tree fled in terror, while the voice in her head exhaled a sigh filled with pleasure and relief. *"Finally. Finally."*

Aya realized that somehow her height now surpassed the tops of the trees. With wondrous emerald eyes, she took stock of herself. Her arms now unfurled into wings and her legs were muscled and strong. She had no idea what her face looked like but she used her large claws to gauge it. She had a snout and a mouth filled with long, razor sharp teeth. *"What am I?"*

The female voice replied, *"Humans name you, Dragon."*

Aya's head swam giddily.

"And now that I have given you my form, I must leave. I've been waiting in my root for the final sleep a very long time."

Aya sensed the dragon's presence drawing away. *"Wait. Please don't go, I have so many questions."*

"All answers can be found in the land behind the veil of Africa's snow topped mountain, so use your wings."

"I can fly home!"

"Of course. But first, burn the male Fire spirit below you so he can be free, too. Then, if you choose lay waste to this terrible place. Good bye, little one."

And she was gone. Aya spent a few moments assessing and appreciating the beauty of her new form, and the unlimited power she sensed it held. *Thank you, Mother.* She turned her attention to Jeremiah standing below her beside the dropped litter. He was the only person who hadn't fled, unless one counted Granger who was doing his best to crawl away on his useless legs.

"Jeremiah!" Her deep voice shook the ground.

He smiled up. "You're very beautiful."

She lowered her head to see his face clearly. "Thank you. I can free you, but I have to burn the body you're in."

"Please."

She had no idea how to do what was needed, but when she opened her mouth a gentle stream of flame cascaded over him as if she'd been wielding it her entire life. Out of the blackened flesh he rose in dazzling, jewel toned flames of his own and disappeared. She wished him well.

Turning her eyes to Granger who now lay shaking with fear, she voiced, "I will let you live if you pledge not to purchase more Africans."

"To hell with you!" was his answer.

Her reply transformed him into a smoldering pile of ash.

From there, she took the dragon mother's advice and laid fiery waste to his land. The only thing she left untouched was the whipping tree out of respect to all those who'd shed their blood there. Granger's captives had fled and she hoped they'd find sanctuary. Surely there were people somewhere in this awful place who believed buying another human being was wrong.

She took flight, and the beauty of her newfound freedom brought tears to her emerald eyes. She couldn't wait to see home. She did a few practice glides and headed east. Far below, she spotted the overseer Sales on the seat of a fast-moving wagon. When he looked up and saw her he whipped the horses to get more speed. It didn't matter. She left him as ash, too, and flew on.

As a way of saying goodbye, she banked low over the town that held the pens and enjoyed the sight of the people below running like ants. The pens held captives, so she spared them but not the nearby buildings or the empty slave ships tied up at the dock in the harbor. Those she burned gladly. She then flew east over the ocean for the answers awaiting her back home in the land behind the veil of Africa's snow topped mountain.

THE END

Discover More by Beverly Jenkins

The Blessings Series (contemporaries)
BRING ON THE BLESSINGS
A SECOND HELPING
SOMETHING OLD, SOMETHING NEW
A WISH AND A PRAYER
A HEART OF GOLD
FOR YOUR LOVE
STEPPING TO A NEW DAY
CHASING DOWN A DREAM

Old West Series (historicals)
FORBIDDEN
BREATHLESS

The Destiny Trilogy (historicals)
DESTINY'S EMBRACE
DESTINY'S SURRENDER
DESTINY'S CAPTIVE

Grayson Family Series (historicals)
VIVID
JEWEL

Historicals
MIDNIGHT
NIGHT HAWK
INDIGO
CAPTURED

WINDS OF THE STORM
SOMETHING LIKE LOVE
A CHANCE AT LOVE
BEFORE THE DAWN
ALWAYS AND FOREVER
THE TAMING OF JESSI ROSE
THROUGH THE STORM
NIGHT SONG
PRISONER OF LOVE (novella)
BELLE (young adult)
JOSEPHINE (young adult)

Contemporary Romantic Suspense
DEADLY SEXY
SEXY/DANGEROUS
BLACK LACE
THE EDGE OF DAWN
THE EDGE OF MIDNIGHT

About the Author

Beverly Jenkins is the recipient of the 2017 Romance Writers of America Nora Roberts Lifetime Achievement Award, as well as the 2016 Romantic Times Reviewers' Choice Award for historical romance. She has been nominated for the NAACP Image Award in Literature, was featured both in the documentary "Love Between the Covers" and on CBS Sunday Morning. Since the publication of *Night Song* in 1994, she has been leading the charge for multicultural romance, and has been a constant darling of reviewers, fans, and her peers alike, garnering accolades for her work from the likes of *The Wall Street Journal, People Magazine*, and NPR.